Rodney,
the Surfing Duck

DAVID METZENTHEN

ILLUSTRATED BY
STEVE AXELSEN

SuPa DOOPERS

sundance

Published by
Sundance Publishing
234 Taylor Street
Littleton, MA 01460

Copyright © text David Metzenthen
Copyright © illustrations Steve Axelsen
Project commissioned and managed by
Lorraine Bambrough-Kelly, The Writer's Style
Designed by Cath Lindsey/design rescue

First published 1997 by
Addison Wesley Longman Australia Pty Limited
95 Coventry Street
South Melbourne 3205 Australia
Exclusive United States Distribution: Sundance Publishing

ISBN 0-7608-1929-7

PRINTED IN CANADA

Contents

CHAPTER 1

Come on, Duck

Things were pretty bad, Jason thought, when the only person around to go surfing with was a . . . duck. Sure, Jason loved the feathery little fellow, but catching a wave with a duck was a drag. Rodney only liked little waves. He was a duck, after all.

Jason walked along the path to the beach. In front of him, glassy waves curled. Behind him, Rodney waddled, then quacked. Jason waited. Rodney lifted his wings like a tired baby lifted its arms.

"Silly duck," said Jason, but he did pick him up and carry him down to the surf.

CHAPTER 2

Smart Surfing

Jason paddled out, Rodney paddled beside him. The water was cold and clear, the duck's call was loud and sharp.

"Quack! Quack! Quack!"

Jason stopped paddling, although he was only about thirty yards from shore.

"Okay, duck," he said. "Go for it."

Rodney turned for the beach, and with a flap of his wings, surfed away on a ripple. Jason could hear him. "Quack-k-k-k-k-k-k!"

Jason surfed in after him. That crazy duck! Not only couldn't he catch a decent wave, but he wouldn't paddle out again by himself, either.

Jason waited in the shallows for the bird. Looking up, he saw two people watching him and the duck from the dunes. He didn't take much notice. He was too busy watching Rodney.

"Okay, duck," Jason said. "This time we'll catch a real wave!"

Jason scooped up Rodney and put him on the front of his board. The dark-eyed duck stood there like some sort of loony surfing mascot.

Ahead, larger waves lifted and broke. Jason paddled through them, rescuing Rodney every time he was washed off the board.

"Quack," Rodney said quietly, perhaps worriedly.

"You'll be all right," said Jason. "We'll let the really big ones go."

Jason and Rodney paddled out beyond the breakers and sat waiting for the right wave. It was beautiful out here, Jason thought. He loved the ocean.

He would've liked to have someone to surf
with, but all his friends from school lived
far at the other end of the beach.

A set of waves was building. Jason let the first four go, watching them charge into shore like big blue buffaloes.

"A bit too big," Jason told Rodney. "We don't want it to be duck overboard!"

They waited.

"Get set!" Jason said suddenly and paddled for takeoff. "Let's go!"

Jason felt the swell lift and carry them forward. Rodney flapped his wings for balance — and now they were surfing, locked into the speed of the moving water.

"Yesss!" Jason yelled.

"Qu-a-a-a-a-a-c-k!" quacked Rodney.

Jason didn't cut loose with any radical turns. Not with the duck on board. He simply had to surf as smoothly as he could, or the duck would get dumped. And Rodney did not like to get dumped. The feathery little fellow hated it!

CHAPTER 3
Big Money, Mean Wave

Jason rode the wave in. Happiness like bubbling, popping foam filled him. He dropped off the board as the wave faded away — and saw the two people from the sand dune jogging toward him. One was a man with a camera, the other was a girl about Jason's age. She carried a bag of equipment. Both wore green canvas vests with lots and lots of pockets.

"Hey, duck boy!" the man called out. "Stop right there."

Jason stood in the shallows, holding his board, with Rodney standing on it.

The man and the girl suddenly had to run back as a wave slithered toward them. The girl skipped away from the chasing foam, but the photographer's shoes were soaked. Jason laughed. The man waved at Jason.

"Hey, kid, bring the bird. I've got an offer to make."

"What sort of an offer?" Jason wondered. The duck was definitely not for sale.

"What I want," the man said, "is for you to catch a big wave, and I'll shoot the duck." He held up the camera. "Shoot the duck! Get it? Ha, ha, ha!"

The girl holding the bag said nothing. She drew lines in the sand with her bare toes. Her hair was straight and white, bleached by the sun. She looked up. Freckles seemed to dance on her cheeks. Her eyes were green like the sea.

"What's the duck's name?" she asked.

"Rodney," Jason said, "because we found him in Rodney Creek when he was small. A cat had gotten him."

"He's a very daring duck," she said. "Larry would like to take some pictures of him on a big wave."

The man with the camera nodded.

"Sonja's right," he said. "On a really big wave. It'd be a great picture. Maybe it would be seen all around the world. A hundred bucks to do it. Now."

The photographer pulled out a roll of fifty-dollar bills. He held out two. Jason looked at the money. He looked at the duck.

Rodney didn't like big waves. Ducks weren't very strong. A dumping wave might break his wing or pound him down onto the board.

"No," said Jason. "He's no good in big surf. It scares him."

The photographer peeled off more bills. Jason saw that Sonja was again looking down at her toes.

"Two hundred and fifty dollars," the photographer said. "It's a lot of money."

It was. With two hundred and fifty dollars Jason knew he could just about buy the secondhand triple fin board that was in the window of the Rodney Creek Surf Shop. Surely the duck could survive catching just one big wave?

"Okay," said Jason. "I'll do it."

"Great!" said the photographer. "You go out, I'll get ready."

"Be careful," said Sonja. "Those waves look pretty mean now."

Jason turned toward the sea. The tide was coming in, the waves were building.

"One wave," Jason said, and held up one finger. "No more."

The photographer nodded. "That's the deal."

CHAPTER 4
Wild Water

Jason took a long time to paddle out
through the waves. Three or four times he
had to rescue the duck from the rough
foamy water. Rodney didn't make a sound.
He simply stood on the board and looked
out at the rising swells.

"One wave," Jason told him, as they made it out beyond the breakers.

Here they were safe. The waves ran underneath them, not steep enough yet to pick them up and fling them toward shore.

But Jason was scared. The waves were tall and powerful, and broke with a booming thump. He waited, thinking about the money — and the duck.

"One wave," he muttered. "Just one wave."

Jason could see a set of waves building. The first swell was big, the second swell was bigger — the third was enormous.

"Action stations!" Jason yelled. "Get ready, duck!"

Jason paddled over the first two waves, but he turned around to catch the third. He could feel it lifting, gathering him and Rodney into its power. Jason was frightened. The wave was a monster. It seemed to want to hurl him and the duck into the sand dunes. Or drown them under tons of crashing water. But now Jason had no choice. He had to surf it.

He shot down the wave's steep face. Behind him he could hear it lifting, rearing up. It was going to dump on them big-time. It was going to pound them to the absolute max. He made a split-second decision.

He crouched, picked up the duck, and threw him upward. The wave broke, falling down on Jason like a huge white weight. Instantly he was smashed off his board and held under. He felt as if his arms and legs were being torn off. He couldn't fight the power. His surfboard was gone. All he could do was try to hold onto his life.

Suddenly Jason's head was above water. He was in a sea of churning foam. His surfboard was being tossed toward the shore. He took great big breaths. He heard a strange noise.

"Quack-quack-quack-quack!"

He looked up and saw Rodney coming in for a splash landing.

"Fly!" Jason yelled. "Back to the beach!" He tried to grab the duck, but Rodney paddled away.

Another wave was coming. All Jason could do was dive under it. He dived and felt it go over him like a train. He surfaced and grabbed another breath. He looked up. No sign of Rodney.

"Quack!"

The duck was right beside him. He'd duck-dived right under the wave like a pro surfer. What a bird!

Jason looked ahead for the next wave. The sea was calm. The set had passed.

"Swim!" Jason yelled, and he and the duck headed into the beach.

CHAPTER 5

A New Deal

The photographer and Sonja were waiting for them.

"What'd you throw the bird up for?" Larry yelled. "I could've gotten a great shot. That wave was a triple-decker doozy!"

"It would've just about killed the duck," Jason said. "I was stupid to even try it. I don't care about your picture or the money." Jason walked away, his board under one arm, the duck under the other.

"Sorry, pal," Jason whispered to Rodney. "I saw all that money and I did something really dumb. I'm sorry. We'll surf exactly where you want to surf from now on."

Jason heard footsteps, quick and light,
coming up behind him. He turned.
It was Sonja. He stopped, she stopped.
She brushed hair away from her eyes.
She held out a fifty-dollar bill.

"Larry wants you to have this."

Jason looked at the money. "I don't want it."

Sonja nodded. "You saved the duck," she said. "You could've ridden that wave, but you got Rodney to fly — and you got crunched."

Jason shrugged. "I shouldn't have taken him out there in the first place. I don't want the money. Throw it away."

"I'll give it to the Rodney Creek Sanctuary Fund," said Sonja. "How about that?"

"Good idea," said Jason, and grinned.

Sonja tucked the money into her jeans pocket.

"Could you teach me to surf?" she asked. "My family just moved here. Larry's my stepfather." She pointed to a house that Jason knew had just been sold. "No," she added, looking disappointed. "No, I'd probably only slow you down. I couldn't go out very far. You'd miss all the good waves."

"Hey, don't worry about that," Jason said quickly. "I'll teach you for sure. Rodney and I love it in the shallows. Everybody's got to start somewhere."

Sonja smiled, then pretended to throw something over her shoulder.

"And no more pictures," she said. "I promise."

. . but I suppose that wasn't the end.

About the Author

DAVE METZENTHEN

David Metzenthen lives in Melbourne, Australia, and tries really hard to write books that most definitely could be true! He is interested in sailboarding, indoor rock climbing, fishing, the environment, and good books. He is married, has two children, and a goldfish named George who eats like a horse. David likes to write stories that contain action, adventure, and ideas about life.

All of the author's books are set in Australia, although David has traveled to Europe and the United States. He hopes that his stories and characters will find a place in your memory, as well as on your bookshelf.

About the Illustrator

STEVE AXELSEN

I was born and grew up in Sydney, Australia.

In 1973, I earned a B.A. in Sociology from Macquarie University. After a brief period of house painting, I gradually found work as an illustrator of children's books, and I've been working in this field since 1974. Interestingly, I have never studied art formally.

I now live in the countryside with my family—my wife, my son and daughter, and my cat and dog. My hobbies include gardening and fairly frequent dog-walking.

My full-time work is illustrating for children. In particular, I do a lot of illustrating for educational publishing houses.